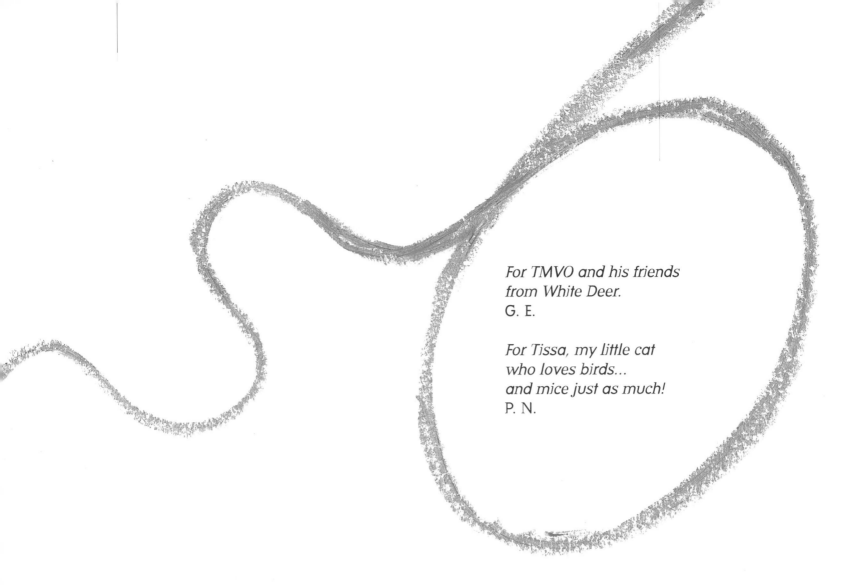

*For TMVO and his friends
from White Deer.*
G. E.

*For Tissa, my little cat
who loves birds...
and mice just as much!*
P. N.

© for the original French edition: L'Élan vert, Paris, 2011
© for the English edition: 2014, 7th printing 2019,
Prestel Verlag, Munich · London · New York
A member of Verlagsgruppe Random House GmbH
Neumarkter Strasse 28 · 81673 Munich

© for the reproduction of the works by Paul Klee: Digital image,
The Museum of Modern Art, New York/Scala, Florence, 2018

Prestel Publishing Ltd.   Prestel Publishing
14-17 Wells Street   900 Broadway, Suite 603
London W1T 3PD   New York, NY 10003

English translation: Cynthia Hall, Stephanskirchen

Copyediting: Brad Finger
Typesetting: Meike Sellier
Production management: Jana Schütz
Printing and binding: TBB, a.s.

MIX
From responsible
sources
FSC® C022120

Verlagsgruppe Random House FSC® N001967
The FSC®-certified paper *Condat Matt Périgord*
was supplied by Papier Union.

Printed in Slovakia

Library of Congress Control Number: 2016937474
A CIP catalogue record for this book is available from the
British Library.

ISBN 978-3-7913-7099-6
www.prestel.com

The CAT and the BIRD

Inspired by a painting by Paul Klee

Text by Géraldine Elschner
Illustrations by Peggy Nille

PRESTEL
Munich · London · New York

I had everything I needed to be **happy**
in my house with the blue shutters.
I had a cozy basket,
warm milk, and toys…

… grass to nibble on,
and a shiny tag on my collar
with my name engraved on it.

But my perfect house
was a gilded cage.
It was **locked up** tight,
the key turned around twice.

So from morning to evening
and from evening to morning,
I sat by the window
and **dreamed** …

The garden outside was so
wonderfully beautiful!

When I closed my eyes tight,
I could sense ... the scent of the chestnuts,
the red leaves of autumn,
the soft carpet of moss beneath my paws,
the murmuring of the stream,
     and, high up in the treetop ... you.
          How beautifully you sang,
               how deliciously beautiful!

For ages I would listen to you
and lick my lips.
I have to admit,
I wanted to catch you very much.
One stroke of my claws,
a snap of the teeth, and ...
crack!

I felt I could already
taste you in my mouth.
Completely.
Forever.

But something inside me
was even stronger
than the urge to devour you.
Deep inside, I envied you.

You were free,
free to fly wherever you wanted,
to come and go as you pleased.
You were free,
and I was captive.

So
I devoured you only with my eyes.
And then I called out to you,
"Hello, bird! Your beak is so sharp,
you can bore holes into the tree trunks.
Why don't you peck at the bars of my prison?"
You answered me with a song.
"A cat in a cage! What a funny sight!
But ... would I be wise to help you?
How can I be sure
that you won't eat me up?"

I looked at you
straight in the eyes and said,
"I give you my word, plain and simple.
And a promise is a promise."

This was enough for you.
Peck, peck!
Without a moment's hesitation,
you began to peck away
the bars of my cage.

And soon I was free,
scampering after you
on the roof of my house with the blue shutters …

... bounding from the tower to the bridge,
and from the bridge to the chimney.
I sprang to the edge of the horizon.
And there I danced for joy

in the moonlight.

"Thank you, little bird!
I will never forget you!"

Your image will always be engraved
in my memory.
Completely.
Forever.

Cat and Bird   painted by Paul Klee

1928
Oil and ink on canvas
38.1 x 53.2 cm
The Museum of Modern Art
New York (USA)

The largest collection of
works by Paul Klee is on
display at the Paul Klee
Center in Bern, Switzerland
www.zpk.org.

Did Paul Klee always want to be a painter?

Paul Klee originally wanted to be a musician, and he learned to play the violin as a child. But in the end he decided to study art. He attended the Kunstacademie (Art Academy) in Munich, where he began his studies by making drawings, caricatures, watercolors, and engravings. Paul's interest in music is reflected in his art. And even though Klee constantly made artworks with both his right hand and his left hand, he never stopped playing the violin every day.

What did Paul Klee paint?

Klee painted reality in his own way. He allowed himself to be inspired by nature, even if he did not transfer exactly what he saw onto the canvas. Paul assembled a large collection of plants that he studied carefully. His pictures contain plants, animals, and fields; and they often feature trees, which were important to him. The artist's famous painting "Magic Garden" (1926) is filled with natural-looking and fantastical plants, some of which are shown as simple areas of color. Even Paul's last name, Klee, is the German word for clover ... a fitting reference to the natural world from which Paul never stopped learning.

Paul

Where did he get his Love of color?

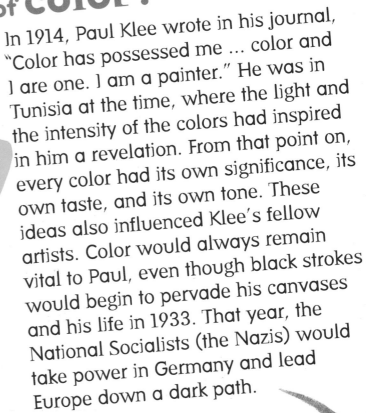

In 1914, Paul Klee wrote in his journal, "Color has possessed me ... color and I are one. I am a painter." He was in Tunisia at the time, where the light and the intensity of the colors had inspired in him a revelation. From that point on, every color had its own significance, its own taste, and its own tone. These ideas also influenced Klee's fellow artists. Color would always remain vital to Paul, even though black strokes would begin to pervade his canvases and his life in 1933. That year, the National Socialists (the Nazis) would take power in Germany and lead Europe down a dark path.